The Three Wishes

ANTHONY BROWNE

PUFFIN

For Andrea

The Three Wishes is inspired by the
story by the Brothers Grimm

PUFFIN BOOKS

UK | USA | Canada | Ireland | Australia | India | New Zealand | South Africa
Puffin Books is part of the Penguin Random House group of companies whose
addresses can be found at global.penguinrandomhouse.com.

www.penguin.co.uk www.puffin.co.uk www.ladybird.co.uk

Penguin
Random House
UK

First published in hardback 2022
This paperback edition published 2023
001

Copyright © Anthony Browne, 2022
The moral right of the author/illustrator has been asserted

Printed in China

The authorized representative in the EEA is Penguin Random House Ireland,
Morrison Chambers, 32 Nassau Street, Dublin D02 YH68

A CIP catalogue record for this book is available from the British Library

ISBN: 978–0–241–52966–9

All correspondence to: Puffin Books, Penguin Random House Children's,
One Embassy Gardens, 8 Viaduct Gardens, London SW11 7BW

FSC
www.fsc.org
MIX
Paper from
responsible sources
FSC® C018179

Lambert, Hilda and Ros were
sat in front of the television.

They were bored and a bit sleepy.

"This programme's rubbish," said Lambert.
"Let's watch something else."

"Oh no – I'm enjoying it," said Hilda. "Keep it on."

"It's like watching paint dry," said Lambert.
"Change the channel!"

"Well," said Ros, "we could turn the TV off and
do something else. Maybe we could go outside?"

Just then . . .

. . . a blue fairy appeared on the screen.
She looked straight at them and spoke:
"LAMBERT . . . HILDA . . . ROS . . .
LISTEN TO ME!"

They could hardly believe their ears –
or their eyes!

The fairy climbed out of the television
and into the room, their room.

"I have a very special gift for you all," she said.

"I'm going to grant you just three wishes – they will all come true, but be very careful what you wish for . . ." Then she was gone.

"YAY! That's fantastic," yelled Lambert. "We can choose anything we want!"

"Wonderful!" said Hilda. "What shall we wish for? Let's think about it first before we do anything silly."

"I'm starving," said Lambert (who always seemed to be hungry). "What have we got in the fridge?"

"Nothing," said Hilda.

"I'd like a **great big** banana to munch on while we decide . . ." said Lambert.

Suddenly the **biggest** banana you've ever seen

appeared on the table.

"You FOOL!" shouted Hilda. "Look what you've done!"
"I didn't know that would count as a wish," said Lambert.
"That's not fair!"

"I wish that blooming banana was stuck on the end of your blooming nose!" said Hilda.

Suddenly it was.

"Oh no!" cried Hilda. "I didn't mean it!"

"Oh nose!" said Lambert, as he tried
to pull the banana off.

He tried and tried, but it was stuck.

Hilda tried to help too, but it wouldn't budge.

They all tried, but they couldn't shift it.

"What have we done?" said Hilda.
"What can we do?" said Lambert.

"There's only one thing we can do," said Ros.

"I wish that
BLOOMING BANANA
would
DROP
OFF
Lambert's nose."

And it did!

For a while no one said anything.

Ros broke the silence. "Well," she said,
"at least we can enjoy the banana now."

They all agreed it was
the best blooming banana
they'd ever eaten.

What would you have wished for?